★ *GREAT SPORTS TEAMS* ★

THE GEORGETOWN

MEN'S BASKETBALL TEAM

Howard Reiser

Enslow Publishers, Inc.
44 Fadem Road   PO Box 38
Box 699   Aldershot
Springfield, NJ 07081   Hants GU12 6BP
USA   UK
http://www.enslow.com

Dedication
We dedicate this book to the memory of Howard Reiser.

The Publisher

Library of Congress Cataloging-in-Publication Data

Reiser, Howard.
    The Georgetown Hoyas men's basketball team / Howard Reiser.
    p. cm. — (Great sports teams)
    Includes bibliographical references (p. 43) and index.
    Summary: Surveys the history of the Georgetown University men's basketball team, covering key players and coaches and some of the best games the team has played.
    ISBN 0-7660-1160-7
    1. Georgetown Hoyas (Basketball team)—History—Juvenile literature.
[1. Georgetown Hoyas (Basketball team)—History. 2. Basketball—History.]
I. Title. II. Series.
GV885.43.G455R45   1999
796.323'63'09753—dc21   98-19229
                                                CIP
                                                 AC

Printed in the United States of America

10 9 8 7 6 5 4 3 2 1

To Our Readers:
All Internet addresses in this book were active and appropriate when we went to press. Any comments or suggestions can be sent by e-mail to Comments@enslow.com or to the address on the back cover.

Illustration Credits: AP/Wide World Photos.

Cover Illustration: AP/Wide World Photos.

CONTENTS

*G*aining position on Hakeem Olajuwon, Patrick Ewing of Georgetown pulls down a rebound. In the 1984 NCAA Championship Game, Ewing outplayed his arch rival.

CAGING THE COUGARS

A hush fell over the Georgetown Hoyas men's basketball fans in Seattle's Kingdome. Two years earlier, Georgetown fans had suffered through a heartbreaking, one-point Hoyas loss in the National Collegiate Athletic Association (NCAA) Tournament Championship Game.

The Showdown

It was the night of April 2, 1984. A crowd of more than thirty-eight thousand had filled the Kingdome for the forty-sixth NCAA Championship Game. The Georgetown University Hoyas would be facing the University of Houston Cougars. Providing extra excitement to the event was the first matchup between Patrick Ewing of Georgetown and Houston's Hakeem Olajuwon—the nation's two best college centers.

Indeed, the personal matchup between Ewing and Olajuwon had captured the attention of the sports world. But it was the Hoyas' excellent depth, teamwork, and defense that could enable the team to capture its first national championship.

The Hoyas would be without senior guard Gene Smith. A great defensive player, Smith had suffered a severe strain to the arch of one of his feet two days earlier, during Georgetown's win over Kentucky. Smith wanted very much to play in the title game against Houston, but after testing the injury, he informed Coach John Thompson before the game that he could not play. "Hardest thing I've ever done in my life," Smith later said.[1]

A Slow Start

With Smith sidelined, Houston jumped off to a quick 14–6 lead by making its first seven shots—all from the outside.

Making early use of Georgetown's depth, Thompson then inserted Michael Graham, a six-foot nine-inch freshman power forward. Graham's aggressiveness helped cool off Houston's hot shooting and sparked the Hoyas to a 16–16 tie. Georgetown then switched to a man-to-man defense. Ewing made three inside baskets, and the Hoyas went ahead, 24–18.

Moment of Concern

Seven minutes forty-three seconds remained in the first half. Georgetown was winning, 27–22. However, Hoyas fans were worried that their team might be on its way to another defeat in an NCAA title game.

They had reason to be concerned. Patrick Ewing, the Hoyas' seven-foot All-American center, had taken

*M*aking his way back up-court, Michael
Graham points to a teammate to thank him
for an outstanding pass.

a seat on the bench. He had just committed his second
personal foul.

With Ewing out, Coach Thompson used a spread
offense. Georgetown increased its lead to 40–30 by
halftime. Contributing to the Hoyas' good fortune was
Olajuwon's own foul trouble—three fouls in the first
half—and his lack of aggressiveness on offense.

Georgetown's Reggie Williams shields the ball from the Bucknell defenders. In the 1984 championship game against Houston, Williams led the Hoyas in scoring.

Only seconds into the second half, Olajuwon committed his fourth foul. Two minutes later, he was removed from the game. "I thought he was playing too cautiously," explained Guy Lewis, Houston's coach.[2]

As Olajuwon watched, the action on the court was fast and furious. While Hoyas freshman Reggie Williams was on his way to scoring a team-high 19 points, Cougars guard Alvin Franklin scored 14 points in less than eight minutes. With more than ten minutes remaining, Georgetown's lead had been slashed to 57–54.

Closing It Out

The Hoyas would not allow the Cougars to get closer. Williams scored off his own missed shot. Graham then made an exciting dunk—two of his ten second-half points. Georgetown was now ahead, 61–54. With less than two minutes remaining, they were leading by eight points. The celebration would soon begin.

"I was afraid when Patrick got two fouls, and I thought I might have left him out too long," said Hoyas coach John Thompson after the game.[3]

Ewing's early foul problems proved to be of no concern. As Thompson spoke, his team celebrated. And no wonder! The Georgetown Hoyas had just become the men's national basketball champions for the first time ever.

"That's our style of play," said Thompson, after his entire team contributed to the Hoyas victory over the Cougars, 84–75. "These players have accepted their roles well. They all made sacrifices to win the national championship."[4]

*T*oday, the Georgetown Hoyas usually play in front of a packed house. In the early days of Georgetown basketball, the team would play to very small crowds.

THE EARLY HISTORY

The players had good reason to feel excited. They were members of Georgetown University's first official basketball team.

A New Sport

It was 1906—fifteen years after the sport of basketball had been invented by Dr. James Naismith. Although few people expected the sport to attract much attention on Georgetown's campus, the excitement and enthusiasm of the Georgetown players was certainly understandable.

"As athletes, the players were eager to show off their basketball talent," said Jon K. Reynolds, the Georgetown University archivist, who keeps Georgetown's records. "Also, they knew that as members of Georgetown's first basketball team, they would always be an important part of Georgetown's sports history."[1]

Humble Beginnings

Ryan Gym was the Hoyas' first home basketball site. It was a small, simple-looking gym. "There were no seats," said Reynolds. "Fans attending games there had to stand. And there was room for only a few dozen people."[2]

Still, Georgetown's basketball players felt especially warm toward Ryan Gym. Some had already played informal games there, and they enjoyed the gym's cozy setting.

Georgetown did not have an official coach in its initial 1906–07 season. Yet in its very first game, Georgetown easily beat Virginia, 22–11, in Ryan Gym. The Hoyas also beat George Washington by two points. Georgetown's record in its first season was 2–2.

Georgetown eagerly looked forward to its second season. Maurice Joyce was hired as the Hoyas' first coach. Joyce is largely credited with having introduced basketball to Georgetown University several years earlier by arranging informal games between Georgetown and other teams. No records of the games were kept.

In Joyce's first game as official coach, the Hoyas trounced Maryland, 58–3, in Ryan Gym. In another game, the team blasted the University of Virginia, 64–12. Over the next four years, Joyce enjoyed vast success as a coach. He also helped create interest among Georgetown students in their basketball team. While baseball and football were the most popular sports at Georgetown, interest in basketball continued to grow over the years. The Hoyas had winning records nearly every season through the 1920s. At

A lonzo Mourning of the Hoyas tries to put a move on St. John's center Robert Werdann. The rivalry between these two schools dates back to the 1909–10 season.

*E*lmer Ripley (far right) led the Georgetown Hoyas to their first-ever appearance in the NCAA championship game.

times, the basketball team was excellent. For instance, Georgetown's record was 22–2 over the 1918–19 and 1919–20 seasons. It then enjoyed records of 10–4 and 11–3 in each of the next two seasons, beating such teams as George Washington, North Carolina, Kentucky, and St. John's.

Student Support

The Hoyas' success helped boost school spirit. The increase in fan support caused Georgetown to move home games from Ryan Gym to larger home court locations. These sites included the Arcade Skating Rink, Riverside Arena, Uline Arena, McKinley Tech High School, and the Washington Armory.

After some twenty-five years of basketball success, Georgetown suffered through six losing seasons

The Georgetown Hoyas Men's Basketball Team

during the 1930s. However, the school went on to twice earn itself a place in basketball history during the early 1940s. It achieved these feats by being part of the first televised college basketball event and, three years later, by reaching the finals of the NCAA Basketball Tournament.

On February 28, 1940, college basketball was televised for the very first time. Station W2XBS carried a doubleheader that included a game between Georgetown and New York University (NYU) at Madison Square Garden in New York City. The Hoyas lost, 50–27.

National Exposure

In the 1942–43 season, Georgetown beat NYU and DePaul to reach the NCAA Tournament final. Among the players on that Hoyas team was Henry Hyde, a future congressman from Illinois. Hyde, with the rest of the Georgetown team, played Wyoming in the title game on March 30, 1943, at Madison Square Garden.

The Wyoming players, on the whole, were taller than the Hoyas. Still, Georgetown led by five points with only six minutes left in the game. However, despite playing an excellent game, the Hoyas lost to Wyoming, 46–34.[3]

The next day, *The New York Times* praised the "magnificent stand" of the Hoyas, coached by the legendary Elmer Ripley. Georgetown's outstanding performance until the final moments of the game "was, indeed, a tribute to Elmer Ripley's aggregation [his ability to get his team to play together]," reported the *Times*.[4] Georgetown finished the season with a 22–5 record.

*S*urrounded by St. John's players, Patrick Ewing looks to pass to an open man. After his career at Georgetown, Ewing was the first pick of the 1985 NBA Draft.

HOYAS HEROES

Dozens of Georgetown University basketball players have earned national acclaim since the Hoyas began the men's basketball program in 1906.

Patrick Ewing

Patrick Ewing is the greatest basketball player in the history of Georgetown University. "He's a warrior," said John Thompson, Georgetown's basketball coach, as the seven-foot center led the Hoyas to national prominence.[1]

A three-time All-American, Ewing began his college career in the 1981–82 season. As a freshman, he led Georgetown to the NCAA title game—the first of three times Ewing led the Hoyas to the final game. In 1984, he was NCAA tournament MVP, as Georgetown won its only national championship.

Ewing was voted America's best college player in 1985. He is Georgetown's career leader in rebounds with 1,316, and in blocked shots with 493, and he ranks second in points scored.

A perennial National Basketball Association (NBA) all-star with the New York Knicks, Ewing is the Knicks' career scoring leader.

Alonzo Mourning, Jr.

Alonzo Mourning was born on February 8, 1970, in Chesapeake, Virginia. He enrolled at Georgetown prior to the 1988–89 season, and led the nation with 169 blocked shots as a freshman. He was voted to the Big East All-Rookie Team and to the All-Big East second team. He was also Big East Defensive Player of the Year.

Starring at power forward the next year, Zo was voted to the All-Big East first team and was Big East Defensive Player of the Year, sharing the honor with teammate Dikembe Mutombo.

As a junior, Mourning was plagued by a foot injury. But as a senior, he won All-America honors at center. He averaged 21.3 points and 10.7 rebounds per game and was second nationally in blocked shots. Zo ended the year with a career average of 3.77 blocked shots per game—the best in Hoyas history.

In the NBA, Mourning has starred with the Charlotte Hornets and the Miami Heat.

Eric "Sleepy" Floyd

He is known as Sleepy. He is also known as the Hoyas' career leader in scoring and steals, and as one of its all-time stars.

*G*eorgetown's Alonzo Mourning is focused on the basket, while Miami's Anthony Lawrence tries to stop him.

Born on March 6, 1960, in Gastonia, North Carolina, Eric "Sleepy" Floyd was loudly cheered by Georgetown fans during his four years as a shooting guard. He also caused opposing coaches to get gray hair.

"He killed me," says Lou Carnesecca, the retired St. John's University coach, laughing. "He was a great player. And what a tremendous shooter he was!"[2]

Sleepy was the Hoyas' career leader with 2,304 points and 253 steals. He was a second-team All-America as a junior in 1980–81 and was a unanimous All-America choice as a senior.

Sleepy Floyd was drafted in the first round of the 1982 NBA draft. He averaged 12.8 points per game in his thirteen-year NBA career, making the All-Star team in 1987.

Dikembe Mutombo

When Bill Russell talked, Dikembe Mutombo listened. The words of the former Boston Celtics superstar made an impression upon Mutombo. Said former New York Knicks coach Fuzzy Levane: "Dikembe became a tremendous defensive intimidator—just like Russell."[3]

Born on June 25, 1966, in Kinshasa, Congo, the seven-foot two-inch Mutombo came to America at the age of twenty-one to play basketball at Georgetown. Within two years, he was a defensive wizard.

In his first season—as a college sophomore in 1988–89—Mutombo developed slowly. The next season, he averaged 10.7 points and 10.5 rebounds per game. He shared Big East Defensive Player of the Year honors with teammate Alonzo Mourning.

As a senior, Mutombo pulled down a school record 389 rebounds and averaged 12.2 rebounds per game. He was again voted Big East Defensive Player of the Year.

Mutombo has starred with the Denver Nuggets and Atlanta Hawks in the NBA. He won the NBA's Defensive Player of the Year Award three times from 1995 to 1998.

Allen Iverson

Born on June 7, 1975, in Hampton, Virginia, Allen Iverson enjoyed a brilliant two-year career at

*T*he Villanova players can only watch helplessly as Georgetown center Dikembe Mutombo slams the ball through the hoop.

Georgetown during the 1994–95 and 1995–96 seasons. His career scoring average of 23.0 points per game and his 124 steals in 1995–96 are both the best in the school's history.

A brilliant ball handler, the six-foot Iverson was Big East Defensive Player of the Year in his two seasons at Georgetown. The following season, he was also voted first team All-America by the Associated Press and United Press International.

In 1996, Iverson was drafted by the Philadelphia 76ers, and he won the NBA Rookie of the Year Award for the 1996–97 season.

*J*ohn Thompson has turned the Hoyas men's basketball program into one of the strongest in the country.

GREAT LEADERS

Georgetown University's men's basketball program has had many excellent coaches and other important people working behind the scenes.

John Thompson

John Thompson knew he faced a difficult task. But he was certain he would succeed. "I know we can win," said Thompson, before starting his first season as Georgetown's men's basketball coach in 1972. "It will just take a little time."[1]

It was not long before Thompson turned what had been a poor basketball team into a major power. In only his third year as coach, he led Georgetown to an 18–10 record. In the years that followed, the Hoyas became a top-ranked team. His achievements included winning a national championship and making three Final Four appearances—all within a four-year period.

Thompson has the highest winning percentage in Hoyas' basketball history for those coaching more than one year. While leading Georgetown to a 596–239 record, Thompson guided his teams to twenty-four straight postseason appearances. Georgetown also had the best overall Big East record and had won thirteen conference titles—also the best in the Big East.

The winner of seven Coach of the Year awards, he is a past president of the National Association of Basketball Coaches.[2]

Mary Fenlon

Mary Fenlon is not famous. But she has been very important in helping the Hoyas basketball team achieve greatness.

Fenlon has served as academic coordinator for Georgetown's men's basketball program, making sure that the players are working toward graduation.

Fenlon was the first person John Thompson hired after becoming head coach. Thompson is proud of his coaching record. But he is equally proud that nearly all his players have graduated from college since Fenlon was hired.

Said Hoyas guard Dean Berry, "My first impression was that Miss Fenlon was a very nice person. She didn't talk about basketball. She talked about grades and schoolwork. That gave me a really good idea about her and how she wanted everyone to get their schoolwork done."[3]

The Georgetown Hoyas Men's Basketball Team

*T*hompson and the Hoyas celebrate after winning the 1987 Big East Tournament.

Elmer Ripley

There is a good reason why Elmer Ripley is one of only two men's basketball coaches in Georgetown's Hall of Fame.

During his ten years as Hoyas coach, Ripley had a record of 133–82 for a .619 winning percentage. He won more games than any other Hoyas basketball coach except John Thompson.

"He was an excellent, inspirational coach," said Red Holzman, who coached the New York Knicks to two world championships.[4]

In all, Ripley coached eight college teams. His teams won 298 games. A member of the famous

*J*ohn Thompson poses with superstar center
Patrick Ewing. More than a coach, Thompson
and his staff work to insure that Georgetown
players will leave the school with a degree.

"original Celtics" as a player, Ripley was elected into
the Naismith Memorial Basketball Hall of Fame in
1972.[5]

Maurice Joyce

Maurice Joyce had a solid record of 32–20 in his four
years as head coach of Georgetown's men's basketball
team. Joyce is mostly remembered for being the first

Hoyas men's basketball coach and for being the key figure behind the starting of a basketball program at Georgetown.

"He was the 'father' of Georgetown basketball, and of basketball in the Mid-Atlantic Region," says university archivist Jon Reynolds.[6]

Joyce, who had been a popular circus acrobat, became the Hoyas' first coach in the 1907–08 season. This was one year after Georgetown began its basketball program. Georgetown had a 5–1 record in Joyce's first season. Joyce had a 9–5 record in his second season, and a record of 5–7 in his third season. In his last year as coach, Joyce enjoyed a record of 13–7.

James Colliflower

James Colliflower was Georgetown's second men's basketball coach. He went on to become one of only two men's basketball coaches—along with Elmer Ripley—to be inducted into Georgetown's Hall of Fame.

Colliflower's four-year Georgetown coaching record was 43–20. His .683 winning percentage was the second best in Hoyas men's basketball history for those coaching more than one year.

Colliflower had an 11–6 record in his first year as coach, in the 1911–12 season. In the next two years, his teams had records of 11–5 and 10–6. Colliflower then left his coaching position at Georgetown. After returning for the 1921–22 season, he guided Georgetown to an 11–3 record.

*S*tanding his ground like a stone wall, Patrick Ewing knocks the ball away from Roosevelt Chapman of the University of Dayton.

AWESOME EIGHTIES

They were NCAA national champions one year. They were narrowly beaten for the national championship two other years. They were Big East Tournament champions three years. They had the best four-year record of any major college basketball team in nearly thirty-five years.

A Dominant Team

They were the Georgetown Hoyas men's basketball teams of 1981–85, led by Patrick Ewing, the three-time All-American center. There was no doubt about it. The Hoyas were one of the best college basketball teams ever.

"They were special," recalls former St. John's University basketball coach Lou Carnesecca. "Georgetown of the early 1980s ranked with the greatest college teams. And they were intimidating!"[1]

1983-84: The Championship Season

Georgetown enjoyed its greatest success during the 1983–84 season. It won its first national championship and finished with a 34–3 record. On its way to the NCAA title, Georgetown was the Big East Conference's regular-season champion, the Big East tournament champion, and the NCAA tournament's West Regional champion. Then, in the Final Four Semifinals, the Hoyas beat the Kentucky Wildcats, 53–40, in a great defensive performance.

Losing by seven points at halftime, Georgetown held Kentucky to three second-half baskets. Leading the effort was senior guard Gene Smith, a defensive star. During the season, Smith played an important role in the Hoyas' holding opponents to an NCAA record-low 39.2 shooting percentage.

"If I keep jumping in your face for 40 minutes, it's going to wear you down," said Smith.[2]

In addition to Ewing and Smith, Hoyas players included Fred Brown, senior guard; Bill Martin, junior power forward; Michael Jackson, sophomore point guard and assists leader; David Wingate, sophomore forward and talented scorer; and Reggie Williams, freshman forward and future All-American. Other players were Ralph Dalton, junior backup center and forward; Horace Broadnax, a sophomore guard who sparked Georgetown off the bench; and Michael Graham, freshman power forward.

Nearly every Georgetown player made an important contribution to the team's championship. In fact, the nonstarters scored 1,040 of the Hoyas' 2,611

The Georgetown Hoyas Men's Basketball Team

*G*eorgetown's David Wingate attempts to block the opposition's shot. Wingate was an important part of Georgetown's great teams of the 1980s, and went on to have a long NBA career.

points during the season. This was 40 percent of Georgetown's total points.

Most basketball experts were not surprised that the Hoyas had won the school its first NCAA championship. Ever since Ewing's freshman season in 1981–82, many had predicted that he would lead Georgetown to the national title.

*E*ric "Sleepy" Floyd is Georgetown's career leader in points scored. Originally drafted by the New Jersey Nets, Floyd made the NBA All-Star team as a member of the Golden State Warriors.

Runners-Up

In Ewing's first season, Georgetown won the Big East tournament and the NCAA Western Regional before losing to North Carolina, 63–62, in the NCAA Final. Led by Ewing and senior two-time All-American Eric "Sleepy" Floyd, Georgetown finished the season with a 30–7 record.

Other players included such talented freshmen as Martin; forwards Anthony Jones and Ralph Dalton; sophomores Gene Smith and Fred Brown; and senior forwards Eric Smith and Mike Hancock.

"We were nationally ranked, yet Georgetown killed us in its first Big East game of the season," recalls Carnesecca. He then laughed, and jokingly added: "They could have beaten Michael Jordan and the Chicago Bulls."[3]

After a disappointing 22–10 record in 1982–83, Georgetown was the next season's national champion. It then set its sights on winning a second straight championship.

The Team to Beat

Judged America's best college team at the start of the 1984–85 season, Georgetown won its first 18 games. Led by Ewing, it went on to win its second straight Big East Tournament, won the NCAA Eastern Regional, and advanced to the Final Four for the third time in four years. But after trouncing St. John's, Georgetown was upset by the Villanova Wildcats, 66–64, for the championship.[4]

Despite their loss to Villanova, Hoyas players were proud of their season's 35–3 record. The Hoyas' 121 wins were the seventh most by a college team over a four-year period.[5]

*J*ohn Thompson has seen many of his players go on to play professional basketball. Othella Harrington (shown here) is one.

POWERFUL PROGRAM

College basketball coaches and other experts agree that Georgetown University has long had one of the very best college basketball programs in America.

A Winning Tradition

They also agree the Hoyas will continue to play excellent ball for many years to come. Entering the 1997–98 season, Georgetown's all-time basketball record was 1,233–777, an outstanding .613 winning percentage.

"John Thompson reestablished Georgetown's tradition of basketball greatness," said Fran Fraschilla, former coach of St. John's Red Storm. "Its style of pressure offense, and pressure defense, will remain an outstanding team trademark. I feel Georgetown will continue to have a nationally ranked team—even after John Thompson has left coaching."[1]

Fraschilla and others praise both Thompson's commitment to education and the importance he places on his players' working hard to earn their college degrees. "Coach Thompson cares deeply about his players, and about their future," said Fraschilla. "This is especially important to the parents of players. Coach Thompson's most important contribution may be that many of his former players have enjoyed great success in [later] life."[2]

Hard Workers

Jim Calhoun, coach of the Connecticut Huskies, described Georgetown's program as having "family values in a basketball setting. No team works as hard as the young men in John Thompson's program. I would expect Georgetown's basketball team will continue to enjoy immense success for many years."[3]

Louis Orr, assistant basketball coach at Syracuse University, predicted that Georgetown would remain a major basketball power by continuing to play "hard, aggressive ball" under Thompson. "Georgetown has successfully combined academics, athletics, and a winning tradition," said Orr. "This success will continue. The biggest attractions to Georgetown basketball are Coach Thompson, and the success he has achieved. His commitment to his players, and to their education, speaks for itself. This loyalty and concern are very important to a parent."[4]

Reloading

As the Hoyas move into the twenty-first century, Georgetown remains an attractive choice for talented

The Georgetown Hoyas Men's Basketball Team

*G*eorgetown's Allen Iverson tries to beat Weber State's Ruben Nembhard to the ball. Iverson was selected as a Sporting News *first* team All-America after his sophomore season.

players. Outstanding new Hoyas recruits are big reasons that Georgetown fans look eagerly to the future. For example, in the span of two seasons Georgetown lost both All-American guard Allen Iverson and Big East leading scorer Victor Page.

*O*uthustling his opponents, Dikembe Mutombo grabs the rebound. Georgetown coaches instill a strong work ethic in all their players.

Thompson brought in a recruiting class that featured both high school and two-year college All-Americans.

Coach Thompson resigned in the middle of the 1998-99 season. Craig Esherick, a former Georgetown player and Thompson's longtime assistant, took over as head coach. Esherick hopes to carry on Thompson's coaching ideals.

A former backup center to Bill Russell on the Celtics, Thompson, when asked about the qualities he sought in a potential Hoyas player, said:

> I look for a kid who can fit into the program athletically and academically. That means, first of all, someone who is concerned about getting an education . . . talent and athletic ability are naturally major factors; but I want someone willing to take on the academic challenges of an institution like Georgetown at the same time he is meeting my challenge to excel athletically. . . . You don't really change people. You find people who are willing to work within the guidelines you've already established . . . I think we look for potential and attitude more than anything else.[5]

Formula for Success

National Football League commissioner Paul Tagliabue, a Hoyas basketball star in the early 1960s, was confident that Georgetown would continue to successfully recruit players having those special qualities. "Georgetown enjoys a great winning tradition, while remaining committed to players' educations," he said. "These are reasons I believe Georgetown will continue to have one of America's best college basketball programs for many years."[6]

STATISTICS

Team Record

The Hoyas History

YEARS	W	L	PCT.	FINAL FOUR	NATIONAL CHAMPS
1906–07—1909–10	21	15	.583	None	None
1910–11—1919–20	100	50	.667	None	None
1920–21—1929–30	88	45	.662	None	None
1930–31—1939–40	79	111	.416	None	None
1940–41—1949–50	111	78	.587	1943	None
1950–51—1959–60	112	122	.479	None	None
1960–61—1969–70	136	102	.571	None	None
1970–71—1979–80	171	110	.609	None	None
1980–81—1989–90	267	70	.792	1982, 1984, 1985	1984
1990–91—1997–98	166	91	.646	None	None

W=Wins   L=Losses   PCT.=Winning Percentage

The Hoyas Today

SEASON	W	L	PCT.	COACH	TOURNAMENT FINISH
1990–91	19	13	.594	John Thompson	Lost in 2nd Round of NCAA
1991–92	22	10	.688	John Thompson	Lost in 2nd Round of NCAA
1992–93	20	13	.606	John Thompson	NIT Runner-up

The Georgetown Hoyas Men's Basketball Team

The Hoyas Today (con't)

SEASON	W	L	PCT.	COACH	TOURNAMENT FINISH
1993–94	19	12	.613	John Thompson	Lost in 2nd Round of NCAA
1994–95	21	10	.677	John Thompson	NCAA Sweet Sixteen
1995–96	29	8	.784	John Thompson	NCAA Elite Eight
1996–97	20	10	.667	John Thompson	Lost in 1st Round of NCAA
1997–98	16	15	.516	John Thompson	Lost in 2nd Round of NIT

Total History

W	L	PCT.	FINAL FOUR	NATIONAL CHAMPIONSHIPS
1,251	794	.612	4	1

Coaching Records

COACH	YEARS COACHED	RECORD	FINAL FOUR
Maurice Joyce**	1907–11	32–20	*
James Colliflower	1911–14 1921–22	43–20	*
John O'Reilly	1914–21 1923–27	87–47	*
Jock Maloney	1922–23	8–3	*
Elmer Ripley	1927–29 1938–43 1946–49	133–82	1943
Bill Dudak	1929–30	13–12	*
John Colrich	1930–31	5–16	*
Fred Mesmer	1931–38	53–76	*
Ken Eagles	1945–46	11–9	None

*NCAA Tournament was not held until 1939.
**There was no official coach for the 1906–07 season.

Statistics

Coaching Records (con't)

COACH	YEARS COACHED	RECORD	FINAL FOUR
Buddy O'Grady	1949–52	35–36	None
Harry Jeanette	1952–56	49–49	None
Tommy Nolan	1956–60	40–49	None
Tom O'Keefe	1960–66	82–60	None
Jack Magee	1966–72	69–80	None
John Thompson	1972–99	596–239	1982 Runner-up, 1984 Champions, 1985 Runner-up

RECORD=Record at Georgetown only.

Ten Great Hoyas

PLAYER	SEA	G	REB	AST	PTS	RPG	APG	PPG
Patrick Ewing	1981–85	143	1,316	128	2,184	9.2	0.9	15.3
Eric "Sleepy" Floyd	1978–82	130	477	355	2,304	3.7	2.7	17.7
Othella Harrington	1992–96	132	983	137	1,839	7.4	1.0	13.9
Allen Iverson	1994–96	67	240	307	1,539	3.6	4.6	23.0
Michael Jackson	1982–86	131	225	671	1,284	1.7	5.1	9.8
Alonzo Mourning	1988–92	120	1,032	138	2,001	8.6	1.2	16.7
Dikembe Mutombo	1987–91	96	823	75	947	8.6	0.8	9.9
Victor Page	1995–97	67	242	130	1,146	3.6	1.9	17.1
Reggie Williams	1983–87	138	886	327	2,117	6.4	2.4	15.3
David Wingate	1982–86	139	494	364	1,782	3.6	2.6	12.8

SEA=Seasons with Hoyas   AST=Assists   APG=Assists Per Game
G=Games   PTS=Points   PPG=Points Per Game
REB=Rebounds   RPG=Rebounds Per Game

The Georgetown Hoyas Men's Basketball Team

CHAPTER NOTES

Chapter 1. Caging the Cougars

1. Malcolm Moran, "Georgetown, Led by Freshmen, Wins Title," *The New York Times*, April 3, 1984, pp. B7, B11.

2. Greg Logan, "Georgetown Is the Final One," *Newsday*, April 3, 1984, p. 96.

3. George Vecsey, "Duel That Wasn't," *The New York Times*, April 3, 1984, pp. B7, B11.

4. John Feinstein, "Georgetown's Pressure Cooks, 84–75," *The Washington Post*, April 3, 1984, pp. D1, D4.

Chapter 2. The Early History

1. Jon Reynolds, university archivist, Georgetown University, July 15, 1997; also, subsequent telephone interviews with author.

2. *Georgetown 1996–97 Men's Basketball Media Guide*, "Records, Game by Game Since 1906," p. 89.

3. Gary K. Johnson, statistics coordinator, National Collegiate Athletic Association, 6201 College Boulevard, Overland Park, Kansas.

4. Louis Effrat, "Wyoming Downs Georgetown to Capture NCAA Basketball Title," *The New York Times*, March 31, 1943, p. 24.

Chapter 3. Hoyas Heroes

1. Howard Reiser, *Patrick Ewing, Center of Attention* (Children's Press, Inc., 1994), pp. 10, 16.

2. Lou Carnesecca, former St. John's University basketball coach, telephone interview with author.

3. Fuzzy Levane, former New York Knicks coach, telephone interview with author.

Chapter 4. Great Leaders

1. *Georgetown Athletic Department Brochure 1997–98*, Bill Shapland, editor. Senior sports communications director; Sport Overviews, Men's Basketball.

2. Georgetown 1996–97 Men's Basketball Media Guide, "Georgetown Hall of Fame, Coaches and Officials," p. 85; "Records, Season-by-Season, Coach," pp. 86, 87; "Game by Game Since 1906," pp. 88–95.

3. Coaches' Biographies, John Thompson, Mary Fenlon, http://www.georgetown.edu/athletics/bball/COACHES.HTM; also, see *Georgetown 1996–97 Men's Basketball Media Guide*, p. 19.

4. Red Holzman, former New York Knicks coach, telephone interview with author.

5. Craig Fink, assistant director of Basketball Hall of Fame, telephone interview with author.

6. Jon Reynolds, Georgetown University archivist, telephone interview with author.

Chapter 5. Awesome Eighties

1. Lou Carnesecca, former St. John's University basketball coach, telephone interview with author.

2. Steve Jacobson, "Smith in Command of National Guard," *Newsday*, April 3, 1984, p. 92.

3. Lou Carnesecca.

4. *Georgetown 1996–97 Men's Basketball Media Guide*, p. 93; Georgetown Office of Sports Information, game notes, 1983–84.

5. Gary K. Johnson, statistics coordinator, National Collegiate Athletic Association, 6201 College Boulevard, Overland Park, Kansas.

Chapter 6. Powerful Program

1. Fran Fraschilla, former St. John's University basketball coach, telephone interview with author.

2. Ibid.

3. Jim Calhoun, University of Connecticut basketball coach, quoted by assistant to Calhoun.

4. Louis Orr, assistant basketball coach, Syracuse University, telephone interview with author.

5. Quotes by John Thompson, Georgetown University basketball coach, quoted to author by Georgetown sports information department. Quotes originally published under title, "An Interview with Coach Thompson," *Georgetown Media Guide*, Basketball, 1986–87, p. 15.

6. Quotes by Paul Tagliabue, commissioner of National Football League, quoted to author by Greg Aiello, vice-president of public relations.

GLOSSARY

All-American—A player who has been voted one of the best in his position in the entire nation. Most All-Americans go on to productive careers in the National Basketball Association.

assist—A successful pass to a teammate that results in a basket for the team.

Big East—An athletic conference made up of thirteen major colleges and universities from the eastern United States. Georgetown is a member of the Big East.

center—Most often the tallest player on the court. His job is to block shots, to grab defensive rebounds, and to make easy shots under the basket.

Final Four—The four teams that reach the semifinal round of the NCAA Division I Men's Basketball Tournament.

man-to-man defense—A system in which every defensive player has the responsibility of covering an offensive player. The defender's sole job is to cover his man, unlike in a zone defense, in which the defender covers an area.

personal foul—An infraction by a player against an opponent, such as blocking or reaching in.

point guard—A player who is usually shorter and quicker than the other players on the court. His job is to dribble up court, run the offense, and pass to an open teammate.

power forward—The power forward should grab most of the rebounds for his team, on both offense and defense. He should have more range and a better outside shot than a center.

rebound—Gaining possession of a missed shot that banks off the backboard or rim. If you grab a shot that your teammate missed, it is an offensive rebound. If your opponent missed the shot, it is a defensive rebound.

regional champion—A team that makes it to the Final Four after defeating all four of its opponents in the NCAA Tournament up to the Final Four.

shooting guard—The best outside shooter on the floor. Shooting guards are usually a little taller than point guards and take a lot of three-point shots.

FURTHER READING

Bjarkman, Peter C. *Hoopla: One Hundred Years of College Basketball*. Indianapolis: Masters Press, 1996.

Douchant, Michael. *Inside Sports College Basketball 1998*. Third Edition. Detroit: Visible Ink Press, 1997.

Fortunato, Frank. *Sports Great Alonzo Mourning*. Springfield, N.J.: Enslow Publishers, Inc., 1997.

Kavanagh, Jack. *Sports Great Patrick Ewing*. Springfield, N.J.: Enslow Publishers, Inc., 1992.

Kerkhoff, Blair. *The Greatest Book of College Basketball*. Lenexa, Kans.: Addax Publishing Group, 1998.

Knapp, Ron. *Top 10 Basketball Centers*. Springfield, N.J.: Enslow Publishers, Inc., 1994.

National Collegiate Athletic Association Staff. *NCAA Final Four Record & Fact Book (1939–1991)*. Chicago: Triumph Books, 1991.

Reiser, Howard. *Patrick Ewing: Center of Attention*. Danbury, Conn.: Children's Press, 1994.

Stewart, Mark. *Dikembe Mutombo*. Danbury, Conn.: Children's Press, 1996.

Vitale, Dick, with Mike Douchant. *Tourney Time, It's Awesome Baby*. Lincolnwood, Ill.: NTC Contemporary Publishing Company, 1994.

INDEX

WHERE TO WRITE

Georgetown University
Athletics Department
Sports Information Office
37th & O Streets NW
Washington, DC 20037

WEBSITE

http://guhoyas.com/
http://bigeast.org/sports/mbball/teams/gae/index.htm